P9-DMW-914

For Popsy

A. L. and D. M.

First edition 2011

Library of Congress Cataloging-in-Publication Data is available.
Library of Congress Catalog Card Number 2010039177
ISBN 978-0-7636-5055-1

11 12 13 14 15 16 17 SCP 11 10 9 8 7 6 5 4 3 2

Printed in Humen, Dongguan, China

This book was typeset in Quercus.
The illustrations were done in watercolor and sepia ink.

Candlewick Press
99 Dover Street
Somerville, Massachusetts 02144

visit us at www.candlewick.com

Tell Me the Day Backwards

Albert Lamb ~ illustrated by David McPhail

CANDLEWICK PRESS

"Let's play that game we used to play last summer," said Timmy Bear as he got into bed for the night. "Let's play Tell Me the Day Backwards."

"Oh, I remember that game," Mama Bear said as she tucked him in. "You start."

"Tonight, before I got into bed, I brushed my teeth in the stream."

"Yes, that's right," said Mama Bear. "That was after we watched the sunset from the top of the hill. And do you remember what happened before that?"

"I remember! Papa Bear brought us a yummy picnic, and we ate supper together."

"And what happened before that?"

"Before that, I lay on top of the big rock, sunning myself. It made my fur get toasty!"

"And before that?"

"Papa Bear had to pull me out of the deep pool in the river."

"Yes, that was terrible," said Mama Bear.

"And before that, I was looking at a big scary fish face under the water," said Timmy Bear. "That was terrible, too."

"It must have been," said Mama Bear. "What happened before that?"

"I ran and jumped off the high, high rock into the deep pool."

"And before that?"

"I was chased by bees, and they were stinging me! I couldn't run fast enough to get away from them."

"And before that?"

"Before that, I was eating some of the most delicious honey in the whole world!"

"And before that?"

"Before that, I discovered an old rotten tree stump with a dusty old beehive hidden inside it."

"And that's when you should have come and found me!" Mama Bear reminded Timmy.

"Yes, Mama. And before that, I was creeping through the undergrowth, just like a crafty fox. But I don't remember anything before that."

"I remember!" said Mama Bear. "Before that, you and I ate a breakfast of lovely ants at the anthill."

"That was yummy, too!" said Timmy Bear.

"And what happened before that?"

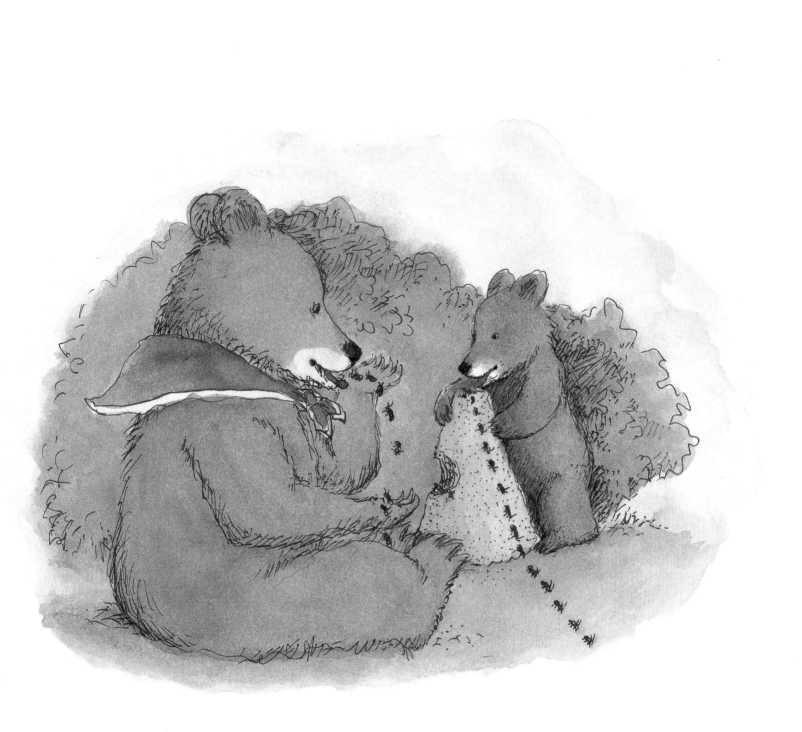

"Before that was early. The sun was just coming up, and you and I stepped out of the cave. We saw all those purple butterflies!"

"And before that?"

"Before that, I think you were sitting by my bed, waking me up."

"Yes," said Mama Bear. "And can you remember the important thing that happened right before that?"

"Before this morning, I slept and slept and slept; you and me and Papa Bear, we slept a deep sleep all through the whole long, cold winter."

"That's right," said Mama Bear. "But tonight we'll sleep for just one night."

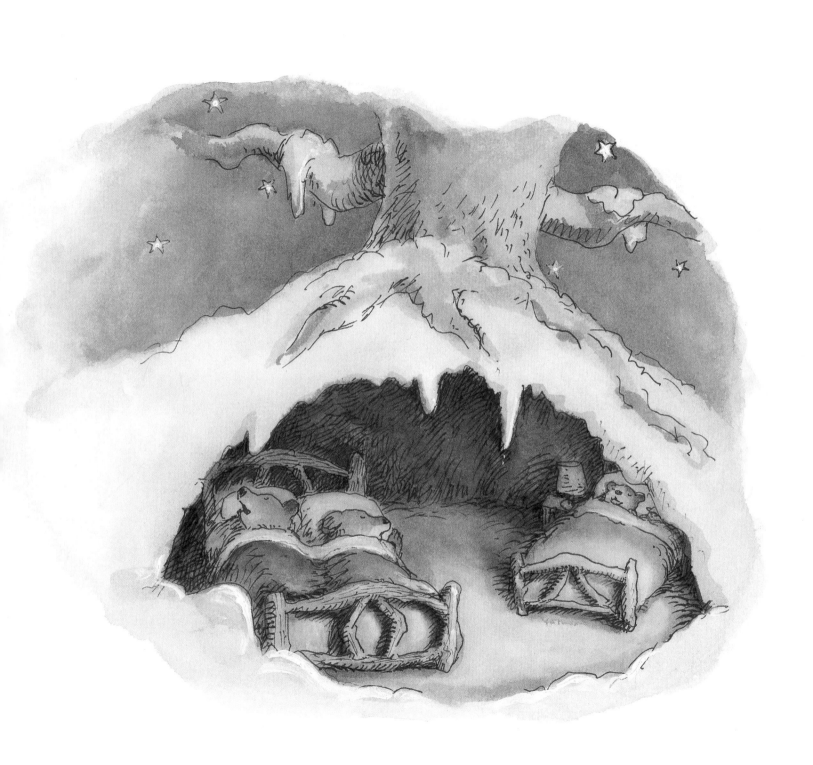

Timmy Bear was very sleepy now.

"Good night, Mama Bear."

"Good night, Timmy. Sleep tight."

Timmy Bear closed his eyes, and soon he was fast asleep.

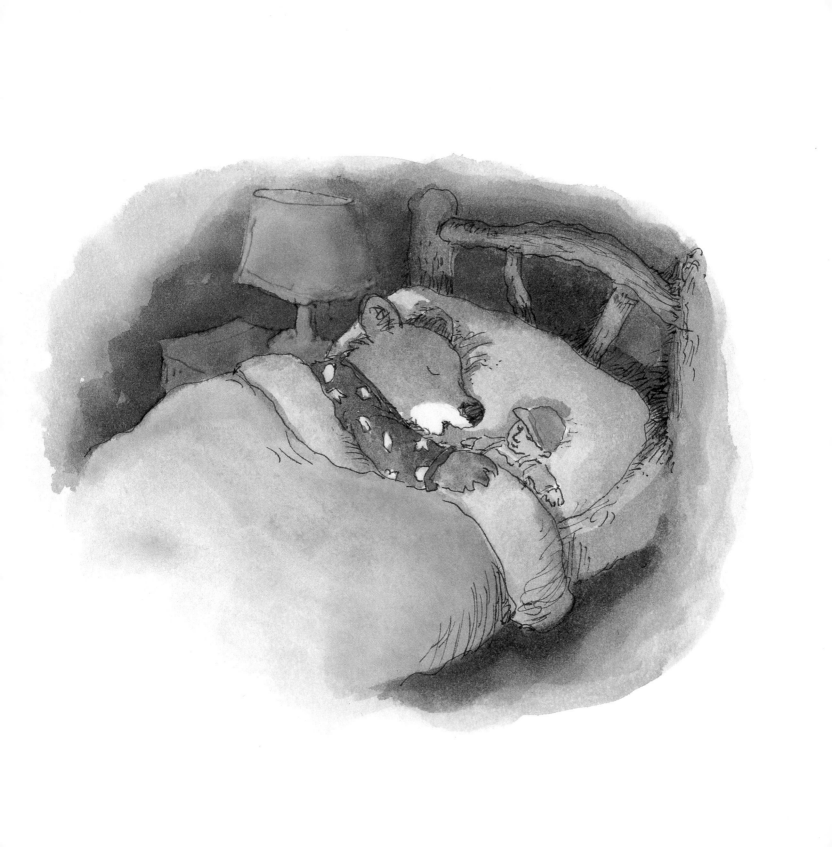